Monsters
in the School

Have you read these books?

❏ The Barnes and the Brains series • Kenneth Oppel
   A Bad Case of Ghosts
   A Strange Case of Magic
   A Crazy Case of Robots
   An Incredible Case of Dinosaurs

❏ *Dragons Don't Read Books* • Brenda Bellingham

❏ *Howard's House is Haunted* • Maureen Bayless

❏ *The Lost Locket* • Carol Matas

❏ *Princesses Don't Wear Jeans* • Brenda Bellingham

❏ *Project Disaster* • Sylvia McNicoll

❏ *School Campout* • Becky Citra

Monsters
in the School

Martyn Godfrey

Illustrations by
Susan Gardos

SCHOLASTIC CANADA LTD.

Scholastic Canada Ltd.

175 Hillmount Road, Markham, Ontario, L6C 1Z7

Scholastic Inc.

555 Broadway, New York, NY 10012, USA

Scholastic Australia Pty Limited

PO Box 579, Gosford, NSW 2250, Australia

Scholastic New Zealand Limited

Private Bag 94407, Greenmount, Auckland, New Zealand

Scholastic Ltd.

Villiers House, Clarendon Avenue, Leamington Spa,
Warwickshire CV32 5PR, UK

National Library of Canada Cataloguing in Publication Data

Godfrey, Martyn
  Monsters in the school

ISBN 0-439-98878-0

I. Gardos, Susan. II. Title.

PS8563.O8165M58 2001   jC813'.54   C2001-930352-1
PZ7.G62Mo 2001

12 11 10 9 8 7 6   Printed in Canada   01 02 03 04 05 06

To my good buddy, Fritz Gagesch.
Thanks for sharing the laughs over the millions of years.

Contents

Chapter 1

Bugging Time

"You guys never listen to me," I said. "Never, ever, never."

"Of course we do, Selby," my mom said.

"No, you don't."

"Yes, we do," Dad said.

"No, you don't."

"Yes, we do," my sister Melissa said.

We were talking during Sunday night Bugging Time. Bugging Time is what my family, the Bennetts, has every night at supper. We tell each other about our day. And if we want to, we get to tell what's bugging us.

I was telling Dad and Mom and Melissa that they never listen to me when I talk. They look at me. They even nod their heads as if they're thinking about what I'm saying. But they don't really listen. They just want me to finish so they can start talking themselves.

They don't listen because I'm the little kid of the family.

I hate that. First, I'm not little. I'm eight years old and in third grade. Second, it's tough when everything you do has already been done by your big sister.

When I tell them what I'm doing in school, it's no big deal. Melissa did the same things when she was in third grade. When I tell them what I'm doing in Brownies, it's no big deal. Melissa did the same things when she was in Brownies.

I even look a lot like Melissa. We both have brown eyes and long brown hair.

The way I see it, being the littlest is the pits. I know that my parents like Melissa the best.

Want proof? When Melissa was a baby, my

parents took pictures of her. There are eight photo albums of Melissa as a baby. Eight! There's one of me. One! It's not even full. And Melissa is in half my pictures.

"I'm going to rob a bank," I said.

"What?" Mom asked.

"I'm going to rob a bank. And when the police catch me, they're going to ask me why I did it. They'll listen to me."

"Now you're being silly, Suds," Melissa said.

Suds is my nickname. I got it when I was three. I dumped a whole box of Mr. Bubble into the tub and turned on the water. The bubbles flooded the bathroom and half the hall.

Melissa wouldn't have called me silly a year ago. She's in seventh grade now, so she thinks she's grown up. She used to play games with me. We played Barbies together. Now she thinks she's a teenager, even though she's still only twelve.

"I'm not being silly," I told her.

But I knew I was, in a way. I'd never rob a bank. But I knew I had to do something to shake up my family. Something that would make them listen to me. Something that Melissa hadn't done.

Melissa and I both go to Spruce Grove School. My teacher's name is Mrs. Boal. (You say it like bowl.) She's okay, but she's kind of old and has bad breath. I told my dad he should buy her some Certs and he told me I was being rude. I think bad breath is rude.

My dad is Mrs. Boal's boss. He's the principal of Spruce Grove School. I like having my dad so close all day. Melissa thinks it's rotten. That's because she's grown up, I guess.

My best friend is in my class. His name is Eric Mercer and we've been buddies since play school.

Eric has an older sister, Crystal. She and Melissa are best friends. He also has a little brother, Karl, who's four. Eric is lucky he's not the little kid.

Eric also has a poodle called Batman. I wish my folks would let me have a pet. But they won't. My mom says she's allergic to pet hair.

That means she starts to sneeze and cry around dogs and cats and hamsters and stuff. I don't think it's fair. If she really knew how much I wanted a pet, she'd put up with a runny nose, wouldn't she?

A little brother and a dog. I don't think Eric realizes how lucky he is.

On Monday I went to Eric's house after school. His mom gave us hot chocolate and cookies. "It's pretty cold today, isn't it?" she asked.

Eric's mom always talks about the weather. I don't think she knows what else to say to me.

"It's really cold," I agreed. I guess I don't know what else to say to her, either.

Eric doesn't have a dad. Well, he does, only his dad doesn't live with his mom. He lives some place in Florida where it's warm all the time. Eric goes to visit him at Christmas and spring break.

I wish I could go to the beach in the middle of winter. We live in White Cliff, Alberta, which is right next to Montana. The United States starts at the end of our schoolyard.

"What do you want to play?" I asked Eric.

He rubbed his hand through his frizzy hair as he munched a cookie. "Let's go in the basement," he said. "I want to show you something."

He and Karl have a playroom down there. Crystal used to play in it too, but she's all grown up this year too.

"What do you want to show me?" I asked.

"Something I built." He smiled. "I want to show you my time machine."

Chapter 2

The Time Machine

"So what do you think?" Eric asked me.

"It looks cool," I told him.

Really I thought it looked stupid. But I'd never say that. Best friends have to know when to tell a white lie.

Eric had put a bunch of boxes in the middle of the playroom. They were held together with black tape. All kinds of wires were wrapped around them. He'd left a space in the middle so you could crawl underneath. It was a real mess.

"It's a great time machine," Eric said. "In a car, train, boat or plane, you can go anywhere you want. In my time machine, you can go any time you want. You want to go back to visit yourself as a baby? You want to see yourself fifty years from now? Just crawl under my machine."

"I don't ever want to be old and wrinkled up like my Grandma Bennett," I said.

"We can go to any time we want," he went on. "Wouldn't it be neat to visit your Mom and Dad when they were our age?"

"I've seen pictures of them," I said.

"This is a real time machine," he said.

"Give me a break," I said.

"Wouldn't it be great if it was?" He grinned. "Wouldn't it be great to go back to caveman times and fight dinosaurs?"

"Mrs. Boal said there were no cavemen when dinosaurs were alive," I told him. "Cavemen came later."

"We could pretend. Or we could pretend to go to the future and be on *Star Trek*. We could meet Mr. Spock."

"He's just an actor," I said.

"How come you're being so sour today?" he asked. "We could pretend."

"I'm sorry, Eric," I said. "I'm grumpy because nobody listens to me at my house."

I told him how tough it was to be the little kid. How nobody in my family paid any attention to me.

"I don't think Karl feels the same way," Eric said. "I think he likes being the little kid. My mother spoils him."

"Maybe my parents should have another baby," I said.

"It's not as great as it sounds," Eric warned.

Karl came down the basement stairs. "What are you playing?" he asked.

"Go away," Eric said.

"Can't make me," he said.

"Selby and I want to play time machine," Eric said. "We want to play alone. Go away."

"Show me your underwear," Karl said.

"What?" I asked.

"If you're wearing underwear and you show

it to me, I'll go." Karl started to giggle.

Eric raised his arm over his head. He made like he was going to hit his brother. "Get out of here, twerp!"

Karl scrambled back up the stairs. "I'm going to tell Mom," he shouted.

"And I'll tell her what you said to Selby," Eric shouted back.

"Underwear?" I asked.

"It's a stupid joke at his play school right now. All you have to do is say the word underwear and he has a fit. He's trying to see as many people as he can in their underwear."

"Why?"

"Who knows?" Eric said. "It's dopey play school stuff. You still want a little brother?"

We looked at each other and laughed.

I played time machine with Eric until I had to go home for supper. During Bugging Time I told Melissa that her toothpaste thing was driving me crazy. It was the ten millionth time I've told her.

Melissa never puts the cap back on the tube.

Every time I go to brush my teeth I have to scrape away dry toothpaste crud. When we use the stand-up tubes, Melissa leaves a lump of paste on the tip. It's gross.

But nothing ever changes. Even though I bug about it again and again, she still does it. Nobody listens to me. So I didn't listen to them either. I sang songs in my head so I didn't have to hear them.

After supper, I went to my room and made a list of things I could do to get my family to notice me.

1. Join a Circus.

The only trouble with that was that I didn't know how to find one.

2. Become a Nun.

I put that down because when Mom gets really mad she says, "Some days I wish I'd become a nun." If she's never been a nun, and I'm pretty sure Melissa has never been a nun, then it could be a good way to get my family to listen to me.

3. Go on a Hunger Strike.

That wasn't such a great idea. I like food too much.

4. *Become a Hermit.*

We read a story in class about some guy who lived in the woods by himself. He didn't want other people around. Mrs. Boal said that someone who stays away from other people is a hermit.

Then it hit me how dumb that was. How could I get them to notice me if I was hiding?

That's as far as I got on my list because Melissa knocked on my door.

"Come on in," I called.

She did. "I'm going over to Crystal's," she said. "I don't know how long I'm going to be. I'll say good night now. You might be in bed when I get back."

"Say hello to Eric for me," I said.

I had a hard time falling asleep. I was still trying to think of a way to make my family listen to me.

Chapter 3

Grats Are Real

The next morning, Brian Butz read another of his stupid stories to me. He's my story-buddy.

Brian Butz is gross.

He says gross things like, "My brother eats worms." And he does gross things. Like when he picks his nose he takes a close look at what he finds.

It's been my bad luck to have Brian Butz in my class since first grade. It's my worse luck to have him as my story-buddy for the whole month of November.

Once a week we have to share the stories we

write in class with our story-buddies. I hate sharing with Brian because all of his stories are gross.

I write about nice things. Pets, birthday presents, friends, stuff like that.

When I finish sharing, he says, "That was dumb. Here's a good story."

His stories are about ninjas chopping up other ninjas. Or monsters eating things. Most of the time, Brian's monsters eat people. Then I have to look at his gross drawings of headless ninjas and half-chewed people. It's awful. I can't wait until Mrs. Boal makes new story-buddies in December.

That day, Brian shared a story about a Grat. He told me that a Grat is a school monster. It lives in the boiler room. Every night the Grat comes out and walks the empty halls. It looks for things to eat.

In Brian's story, the Grat ate the Brownies who were meeting in the gym.

"So what do you think?" he asked when he was finished.

"I think it's stupid," I told him.

"You can't say that," he whined. "Mrs. Boal says you can only say nice things. If you can't say something nice about my story, don't say anything at all."

"You called my story dumb," I pointed out.

"That's different," he said.

"Is not."

"Is too."

"Is not."

"Is too."

"Selby and Brian," Mrs. Boal called. "This is a time to share, not a time to argue."

"Your writing is okay," I said. "It's just the idea that's stupid. Nobody is going to believe in Grats. Monsters don't live in the boiler room of schools."

"It's true," he said. "My mom showed me a story about them in her *Tattle Tale*."

"You're lying."

"Am not."

"Are too."

"Am not."

"Selby and Brian!" This time Mrs. Boal shouted at us. "Share!"

"My mom says that everything in *Tattle Tale* is true," he said. "Grats are real. So there."

I'd seen *Tattle Tale* a couple of times. It's one of the papers they sell near the check-out at the supermarket. The ones with stories about Elvis working as a garbage man in Quebec, or about two-headed aliens that live in your car. Things like that. Most of it can't be true.

Then again, I thought, why would they write it if it wasn't true? Maybe there really is such a thing as Grats. But wouldn't Dad have told me about them. He's a principal. Principals would know about Grats.

The truth is, I have a hard time with monsters. I know they aren't real. But that doesn't make me feel any better when it gets dark. I still have a night light. And I make sure I don't leave my dirty clothes on the chair. One night last year I woke up and my jeans looked like a blobby monster getting ready to jump on me. I started crying.

I always make sure that my closet is closed. I've done that since I was three and Mom read me a book about monsters who like to live in closets. And I still won't go to the toilet in the middle of the night. Even if I have to go really bad, I wait until morning.

When I was little, I used to think there was a toilet monster. I thought when you sat on the toilet seat in the middle of the night it would reach up and grab you. Now that I'm in third grade, I know there's no toilet monster. But I'm still careful.

I don't feel *too* silly, though. Melissa still sleeps with the teddy bear she had as a baby. And she says she's grown up.

"I played a neat trick on my sister and your sister last night," Eric told me as we ate lunch.

"What?"

"You know how Batman falls asleep when you rub his tummy? Well, I took Batman into Crystal's room when she wasn't there. I put him under her bed. Then I rubbed his tummy until he fell asleep."

"Great trick," I said.

"That's not all. When Melissa came to visit Crystal, I told her I'd used my time machine to send Batman a little way into the future. He'd show up anytime. But I didn't know in what part of the house he'd show up. Just that he would."

"And?"

"And they went in Crystal's room." He grinned. "When they started talking, they woke up Batman. He really surprised them. They didn't know where he came from. They think he came out of my time machine."

"Really," I said. "They think that?"

"Maybe," he said. "They might think my time machine works."

"Hmm," I smiled. "That gives me an idea . . ."

Chapter 4

The Great Plan

I didn't get a chance to try out my plan for two weeks. That's because the seventh grade classes were putting on a play for the parents. It was all my family talked about for days.

So I waited until the play was over. And while I was waiting, I told my family about the time machine Eric had built. I had to tell them lots of times because they never listen.

I also told them how Eric had sent Batman into the future, and that he was going to send me. I had to tell them lots of times because they never listen.

I started the plan on a Tuesday afternoon.

Mrs. Kropp is the Spruce Grove School secretary. She has a neat smile. She smiled at me as I walked past her desk.

"How was your day, Selby?" she asked.

"Real tough," I told her. "I'm glad it's over. I had a math test."

I went into my dad's office. And, lucky for me, he wasn't there.

It's great being the principal's kid, I thought. I can just walk into this office. Nobody asks me why. I bet Mrs. Kropp thinks I'm just waiting for a ride home. (I do that if Dad leaves early. Most of the time he stays to work, though. So I walk.)

But I didn't want a ride. I sat down in Dad's chair. His big black date book was where it always was: on top of his desk. I turned the pages until I found tomorrow's date.

Dad writes notes to himself in his big black date book. He writes down the stuff he has to do each day. Maybe he worries that he'll forget his principal things if he doesn't.

I read what was in the book for Wednesday:

1. *Order new basketballs.*
2. *Have Mr. Musgrove check heater in girls' change room.*
3. *Announce bake sale on Friday to raise money for new library books.*

That's it, I thought. I can use the bake sale.

As I left the office, Mrs. Kropp smiled at me again. "I don't know where your father is. Is there something you want me to tell him?"

"I was just going to show him how well I did on the math test," I said. That wasn't a lie. If he'd been in the office, I would have. "Tell him I'll see him at home."

I played at Eric's house before going home for supper. I told him my plan.

"Sounds good," he told me.

"It'll be super," I said.

When Bugging Time came, I was ready.

"And how was your day, Suds?" Mom asked. "Anything you would like to tell us?"

"Melissa left the top off the toothpaste again," I said.

"Sorry, Suds," Melissa said. "I'll try to remember from now on."

"If you listened to me at Bugging Time, you wouldn't forget."

"I wish you would stop saying that," Mom said. "We do listen to you."

"Do not."

"I'm not going to start that again," Mom said. "Is there anything else you wish to share?"

"I played with Eric's time machine after school," I said.

"That's nice." Mom smiled at me.

"Eric sent me into the future. He sent me to tomorrow," I went on.

"That's nice," Mom said again.

"Honest. It's true. I got sent to tomorrow."

"You say that like you believe it," Melissa said.

"I do. It's true. I was in tomorrow."

Mom's smile turned into a gentle frown. "Selby, don't let your imagination get the better of you."

"It's true," I said.

"Selby, enough," Dad said in his principal voice. "We talk about what really went on in our day at supper."

"I can prove it," I told everybody. "I can tell you what Dad is going to tell the kids at school tomorrow."

"Stop being silly," Mom said.

"I think this is fun," Melissa said. "Go ahead, Suds. Tell us what Dad is going to do tomorrow."

Mom, Dad and Melissa stared at me. They were waiting for what I was going to say next. They wanted to hear what I had to say. They were listening to me. My plan was working.

I spoke slowly so I could enjoy it. "Dad is going to tell everybody that Spruce Grove School is going to have a bake sale on Friday."

Melissa and Mom looked at Dad. My father's eyes opened wide. "How did you know . . ." he said.

"Is that right?" Melissa asked. "Is that what you're going to do?"

"A bake sale?" Mom wondered. "You haven't

said anything about a bake sale for the school."

"That's because I just got the idea this afternoon. I thought it would be a good way to raise money for . . . "

I stopped him. "I know what you're going to use the money for."

"You do?" Melissa and Dad and Mom said together.

I grinned and nodded. "Of course I do. I've been to tomorrow. I went in the time machine."

"What's the money for?" Melissa asked.

"Library books," I said.

"But . . . " Dad said in a soft voice. "How could you know that?"

Melissa was wearing a big smile. "Is she right, Dad?"

He nodded.

"All right!" Melissa said. "Great trick, Suds. That was great."

"The only person I told was Mrs. Kropp," Dad said. "Did you hear me talking to Mrs. Kropp?"

"The time machine," I said. "I was in tomorrow."

"Selby, I want to know how you found out. I want to know the truth." Mom sounded upset.

"Come on, Mom," Melissa laughed. "Don't get like that. It doesn't matter how she found out. It was a great trick."

"And you guys listened to me," I said.

"You must have heard me telling Mrs. Kropp," Dad said.

"You listened to me this time," I said again.

"All right," Mom said. "We'll let you keep your secret, Selby. But it's most odd."

Chapter 5

It's a Mystery

I sat down at the kitchen table the next morning and looked over at Melissa. "What's for breakfast?" I asked.

"Mom's junk," she grumbled. "It's like eating tree bark."

That's what Melissa calls the cereal Mom made last week. Mom says it's better for us than Corn Flakes.

My mom thinks a lot about what's better for us. Melissa thinks Mom is a "health nut."

Maybe she is. She goes to a gym class. She also works out with those dance shows on TV where you bounce up and down.

And Mom only eats "health nut" foods. Things with lots of veggies. She never has a Big Mac or french fries.

Lucky for us, Dad eats real stuff. If he didn't, we'd end up eating veggie things all the time.

I don't mind Mom's cereal. It's like granola only it's got fruit and something called dried yogurt in it. It's not as gross as it sounds.

"Where's Mom and Dad?" I asked Melissa.

"Dad's gone to school already," she told me. "And Mom is in the den. Someone called about a house."

Mom is a lawyer. She helps people when they buy land.

I got a bowl and poured some of Mom's cereal.

"Say, Suds, that was really great at supper last night," Melissa said. "You know that stuff about the time machine. How did you do that?"

"It's a real time machine," I told her.

"Right," Melissa said. "And I'm the Queen of England. Tell me the truth. How did you do it?"

"It's a secret."

"Come on. You can tell your best sister."

"You're my only sister," I pointed out.

"Please."

"It's a secret," I insisted.

"Pretty please."

"No."

"Pretty, pretty please."

"No."

"Pretty, pretty please with a cherry on top."

"No."

"Okay," Melissa said. "But I won't play Barbies with you ever again."

"You don't now," I told her. "You haven't played Barbies since you started seventh grade."

"Maybe I will if you tell me how you found out about the bake sale," she wheedled.

"It's a secret."

"You're turning into a real hard case." Melissa smiled at me.

I smiled back. I really like Melissa. Even if she doesn't listen to me.

"Say, Melissa," I said. "You ever think what it would be like if we had a baby sister? Or a baby brother. You ever think what it would be like if Mom and Dad had a new baby?"

"Not really," she said.

"I think about it," I told her. "I think it would be nice if I wasn't the little kid."

She reached over and mussed up my hair. "Enjoy it. Mom and Dad still think you're cute."

"What do you mean?"

"Well, you can still get away with stuff," she said. "If you make a mistake, it's okay. You're the youngest. If I make a mistake, it's awful. I'm a big kid and I should know better."

"I don't know," I said. "I always feel like everyone thinks I'm too little and dumb to pay attention to."

"No," Melissa said. "You're really cute. And that time machine trick was really smart. Really, really smart."

"If I'm so smart, how come you don't listen to me at Bugging Time?"

"I do listen," she said.

"Do not."

"Do too."

At lunchtime I told Eric what had happened at supper the night before.

"They listened to me when I told them about the time machine," I grinned.

"Do they think I made a real time machine?" Eric asked.

"Of course they don't," I said. "They're not stupid. But they don't know how I found out about the bake sale. It's a big puzzle."

"What are you going to make for the bake sale?" Eric wanted to know.

"Nothing. I hate cooking and baking and stuff like that."

"Oh," Eric said. "Well, our family is going to bake cookies. Hey, you going to computer club after school?"

"You bet," I told him. "But I'm going to be a little late. I have to go check my father's date book first. I want them to listen to me at supper."

Eric thought about that. "You know, Selby, that's spying. You're being sneaky and nosey. In a way, it's not right."

"But they listen to me," I said.

"It's still not right."

"There's nothing wrong with it."

"Think about it."

So I did.

"There's nothing wrong with it," I said.

Chapter 6

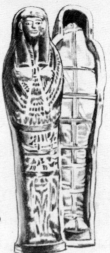

Grats, Mummies And Guts

W e had to write a story in class. That meant I had to share mine with Brian Butz again.

I wrote about a little, lost kitten who was found by a girl. Even though the girl's mom got a runny nose from cats, she let the girl keep it. It was a great story.

As soon as I was finished reading, Brian made farting noises with his armpit. "That's what I think of your stupid story," he said.

I got so mad I told Mrs. Boal. I don't like to snitch but that was too much.

"Brian," she said. "That was rude. How would you like it if Selby did that to you?"

"I'd never do that," I said.

"I know you wouldn't," Mrs. Boal said. "I'm only saying that so Brian gets an idea of how rude it is."

"It wouldn't bug me," Brian said.

"I think it would," Mrs. Boal pointed out.

"But I'd never do that," I said again.

"I know that, Selby."

"I just don't want you to think I'd be that rude."

"I don't want you to do it again," she said to Brian.

I went back to the work table and sneered at him.

"Snitcher," he said.

"Grosser," I said.

"Ugly."

"Stupid."

"Weiner."

"Fathead."

"Brian and Selby," Mrs. Boal called. "Stop

that and share your stories."

Brian picked up his book. "Now *this* is a good story," he said.

It was about a bunch of Grats. They came out of the school boiler room during the Christmas Play. They ate all the parents.

"That was really, totally, all the way dumb," I told him.

"Maybe a Grat will eat you one day," he said.

I was glad when the bell rang at 3:30.

Mrs. Kropp smiled at me as I walked past her and went into my father's office.

To my surprise, my dad was sitting at his desk. "Hi, Suds," he said. "What's up?"

"Not much," I answered. "I just wanted to know if you were going home early tonight? I was going to catch a ride."

"I have to work," he told me.

Now what was I going to do? I couldn't look through his date book with him sitting there.

"What's new in class?" he asked.

"Brian Butz made armpit farts at my story," I said.

"He what?"

Then I saw that Dad's date book was open. He was writing in it.

"Mrs. Boal told him it was rude . . . "

What was he writing?

" . . . but I don't think that . . . "

It was so hard to read upside-down.

" . . . Brian was sorry, he's so . . . "

What did it say?

New office computer at lunch

Aha! That was it. I could use that during Bugging Time tonight.

" . . . gross. I wish I wasn't his story-buddy."

"Maybe I should have a talk with Brian," Dad said.

"I don't think it would do any good. He's too stupid."

"Selby," Dad said in his stern, watch-it-or-else voice. "I don't want you to talk like that about anybody."

"Sorry," I said, even though I wasn't. "I think

I'm going to play in the time machine with Eric before supper. Okay?"

"Fine," he said. "You can tell me what I'm going to do tomorrow."

"Sure thing," I said, and I ran to catch up with Eric.

When we got to Eric's house we went down to the playroom and sat under the boxes. We were in the middle of the time machine.

"Let's go back in time to old Egypt," Eric said.

"I don't know anything about old Egypt," I told him.

"You know, pyramids, mummies and stuff. I know all about it. I read a book on it."

"I once saw a movie where a mummy came back to life," I said. "It was really scary. I stayed awake half the night because I thought there was a mummy in my closet."

"I read how they turned people into mummies."

"I once saw a mummy with my Grandpa Gordon in some museum in Toronto," I told him.

"It took days to turn someone into a mummy," he said.

"You think a mummy could come to life again for real?" I asked.

Eric shook his head. "No way. Mummies are all dried up. And they got no insides. The old Egypt guys took out all their guts. They did that before that wrapped them up."

"They took out all the guts?"

He nodded.

"Mummies have no guts?" I asked.

"They took them out."

"What did they do with the guts?" I asked.

"They put them in jars."

"They put them in jars?"

He nodded.

"What did they do with the jars?" I asked.

"They put them next to the mummy when it was buried."

"You're just making this up," I said.

"Am not. I read it in a book."

"That's gross then. Brian Butz would like that."

"Want to hear something really gross? Want to hear what they did with the brains?"

"No thanks," I said. "I'm pretty grossed out already."

"So, you want to pretend we're in old Egypt?"

"Let's not," I said. "Let's pretend to go somewhere they don't put guts in jars."

"My mom says that's what hot dogs are made of."

"What?" I asked.

"Guts."

"Get real. Hot dogs aren't made of guts," I scoffed.

"Crystal says so, too," he insisted.

"I don't believe it."

"I do," he said.

"Do you believe in Grats?" I asked.

"What's that? Some kind of bug?"

"It's a monster that lives in schools. It lives in the boiler room and only comes out at night. It eats people. Brian told me about it."

"Butz is full of it," he said. "There's no such thing as monsters."

"Right," I agreed. "And mummies can't really come to life."

"Right." He smiled.

"Let's talk about something else," I said. "If we talk about mummies and monsters any more, I'm going to be awake all night."

Chapter 7

Fat, Smelt and Real Boys

Mom passed around the plate of pork chops. I took two.

"You must be hungry tonight," Dad said.

I nodded. "I've been going to all kinds of times with Eric."

"Hey, Mom," Melissa said. "These pork chops don't look right. They're too small or something."

They did look funny.

"I cut off all the fat," Mom said. "It's not good to eat too much fat."

Melissa groaned. "But I like the fat. That's the best part. First I have to eat beaver food for breakfast and now you wreck my supper."

"I am only doing what I think is best for us," Mom said.

"A little fat never hurt anybody," Melissa said.

"I like the fat too," I said. "I like it when it's really crisp."

Mom's face went all tight. "Fine. Next time, I'll leave the fat."

"How was your day, Suds?" Dad asked. "Anything you want to bug about?"

I could tell he wanted us to talk about something else besides fat.

"I had a good day," I told everyone. "Except for Brian Butz."

"What did he do?" Melissa wanted to know.

"I'll tell you after. It's kind of gross. I don't want to talk about it while we're eating."

"That would be best," Dad agreed.

"I went to tomorrow again in the time machine." I tried to say it as if it was no big deal.

"This time machine thing is silly," Mom said. "You sound as if you really think it works."

"What's going to happen tomorrow?" Melissa asked.

"Mrs. Kropp gets a new computer for the office," I said.

"How did you know that?" Dad asked. "How could you know? The store just called me this afternoon. They said they're going to bring the new computer tomorrow at . . . "

"Noon," I said. "I know. I've been to tomorrow."

Dad looked amazed. "There is no way you could know that. I didn't even tell Mrs. Kropp."

"Way to go, Suds," Melissa said. "That's great. You did it again."

And you're listening to me again, I thought.

Mom didn't look amazed. She looked worried. "This is most odd. Maybe we should go over and take a look at this time machine."

Melissa started to laugh. "Did you hear what you just said, Mom? You want to go over and look at something that Eric built. Eric is in third grade. Do you think Eric made a real time machine?"

Dad started laughing too. "That is silly."

"How is Selby doing it then?" Mom asked. "How does she know what's going to go on tomorrow?"

"Who knows," Melissa said. "I don't really want to find out. I mean, it's more fun if the trick is a secret, isn't it?"

"I guess so," Mom said. She didn't sound all that sure.

The next day I stopped at the office on my way to the lunch room. When I walked in I saw a man in a white suit like doctors wear. "O-K COMPUTER WORLD" was printed on his back.

I watched him hook up a computer on Mrs. Kropp's desk. It was just the way dad wrote in the date book. *New office computer at lunch.*

The man turned around and stared at me. He was pretty scary-looking. He had big thick eyebrows and large black eyes. His top lip was

pulled back in a snarl.

"What are you looking at, kid?" he growled. His voice was just as scary. Kind of like his throat was full of dirt.

I just stared at his black eyes.

"Go away," he growled again. "I hate having little punky kids looking at me. Beat it!"

I did.

I ate lunch with Eric. We'd both bought a hot lunch. It tasted awful.

The school cook is Mrs. Welch. She makes weird things out of liver and other stuff that nobody likes. Today's lunch was macaroni and smelt.

"This is lousy," Eric said. "What's smelt, anyway?"

"It has to be some kind of fish," I said. "It sort of looks like a fish. And it smells like fish. I guess that's how it got its name."

"I guess. It stinks."

"Just eat the macaroni," I said.

"The whole thing stinks."

"Mrs. Welch's food makes Melissa really

mad," I told him. "She always bugs about it during Bugging Time."

"Is Melissa in love?" Eric asked.

"Huh?"

"I saw her walking with a seventh grade boy," he said. "They were holding hands."

"No, they weren't. Melissa doesn't hold hands with boys."

"She does so," Eric said. "I saw it."

"Does not."

"Does so."

"Does not."

"Does so. I saw them in the hall," he insisted.

"You really saw them?" I was amazed.

He nodded. "Why would I lie about it? I saw them."

"Did they kiss?" I asked.

"I didn't see."

"Wow," I said. "I guess she is grown up."

"Smelt smells," Eric said.

"You ever think you'll want to hold hands with a girl when you get older?" I asked.

"Yuck," he answered.

"That's the way I feel about boys," I told him. "I hate boys."

He thought about that. "I'm a boy," he said.

"Yeah, but you're not a real boy."

"I'm not?"

I shook my head. "No. You're my friend. A real boy is someone like Brian Butz. Real boys are jerks."

"I'm not a real boy?" He didn't sound happy to hear the good news.

"If you were a real boy, I wouldn't be your friend."

He scratched his frizzy hair. "I'm not a real boy?"

"Am I a real girl?" I asked. "Am I like the other girls in the class?"

"No," he said. "You're Selby. You're okay."

"There you go, then," I said. "That's why we're buds. We're not real."

He scratched his hair a little harder.

Chapter 8

A Washout?

After school I went down the hall to the office again. I had to check Dad's date book for Bugging Time.

Mr. Musgrove, the janitor, was setting up tables in the hall.

"Hi, Mr. Musgrove," I said.

"Hi, Selby," he said. "How's it going, man?"

Mr. Musgrove calls everybody "man." Mom says that's the way hippies used to talk. A hippie was a person with long hair who lived a long time ago. They went extinct, like the dinosaurs.

Mr. Musgrove has long hair with lots of grey.

He ties it in a ponytail. He also has a thick, grey moustache.

"What are you doing?" I asked Mr. Musgrove.

"I'm setting up tables, man," he told me.

I could tell that much. Maybe he thought I looked stupid.

"Why?" I asked.

"For the bake sale things," he said. "You guys brought in so much stuff, like, they can't keep it in the staff room. Isn't that far out?"

"There's a lot, huh?"

"A lot. There's more than a lot. There's a city of cakes and pies, man."

"My dad said he's going to bake a cake tonight. He bought a cake mix in a box," I told him.

"Far out," he said. "When the rest of you bring in your stuff, there will be more."

That made sense.

"Where will we put it all?" he went on. "Think about that, man?"

"But we're going to buy the things tomorrow," I said. "Then we'll eat it."

He smiled at me. "Hey, it's been great talking to you, man. But I've got to work."

He went to get another table, and I wandered into the office.

Mrs. Kropp looked really happy with her new computer.

"This is great," she told me. "This will make my work so easy."

"It looks like it costs a lot of money," I said.

She nodded. "It does, but it's worth it."

"That sure was a mean man who set it up," I said.

"He was, wasn't he?" she agreed. "He didn't seem to like his job at all."

"He scared me," I said.

"Oh, well." She smiled. "Did you want to see your father?"

"Yes," I told her. Or his date book, I thought.

"You can't," she told me. "He's meeting with Mrs. Bompas from the school board. He said he didn't want to be interrupted."

"What's that mean?"

"He doesn't want anyone knocking on the

door," she said. "No phone calls and so on."

"Oh."

"He also said that it was going to be a long meeting," she said.

"Oh."

"Maybe you should walk home."

"I guess," I said. "But I have to see . . . "

I stopped really fast. I almost told her that I wanted to see his date book.

Now what was I going to do? How was I going to get my family to listen to me during Bugging Time?

I didn't have much time to think about it. Thursday night is always a rush for our family.

Mom goes to a class at the college. She's trying to learn how to speak French.

Dad is a member of the Kiwanis. They meet every Thursday.

I get babysat by Melissa.

We always have an early supper on Thursdays. Just as I expected, Bugging Time was a washout. Nobody listened to me.

"Tell us what we're going to do tomorrow,"

Melissa said. "What did you see in the time machine?"

"Eric and I didn't play with the time machine," I said. "I didn't have time to go to his house because of early supper."

"Oh well," Melissa said. "Let me tell you what Steve Butz did in class today. He's so gross. We were looking at worms for Science and . . . "

I had to get them to listen to me again, but I didn't know how. Then Melissa gave me an idea.

As we were cleaning away the dishes she said, "Is it okay if I go over to Crystal's house for a while? We want to make some cookies for tomorrow."

"What about Selby?" Mom asked.

"She can come with me," Melissa said. "She can play with Eric. We'll be back by eight. Honest. I'll make sure Selby goes to bed right away."

"And I'll play with the time machine," I told them. "I'll go to tomorrow."

"Can we go?" Melissa asked again.

"I guess so," Mom said.

"We trust you," Dad told Melissa.

Maybe I should tell them that she holds hands with boys, I thought.

As Eric and I sat in the boxes of the time machine, I worked on my plan.

"How are you going to tell your family about tomorrow? You didn't see your dad's date book," Eric said.

"But I will," I told him. "I'm going to tell them at breakfast."

"How are you going to do that?" he asked. "You can't get into the school until tomorrow."

"Wrong," I said.

"Wrong?"

I took a key out of my pocket. "I took this from the kitchen drawer. It's a key to Spruce Grove School. My dad has a couple of extras."

"What are you going to do with it?"

"Go to the school." I smiled. "We'll go check the date book right now."

Chapter 9

In the Dark

"We're going to do what?" Eric asked.

"We're going to go to the school to read my dad's date book."

"How are we going to do that?" he wanted to know.

"Easy," I said. "We walk to school. We open the door with this key. We go to my dad's office. We read his book. Then we walk back to your place. It won't take more than fifteen minutes."

He twisted some of his frizzy hair around his finger. "You're not kidding?"

"Of course not."

"You're not trying to joke me?" he asked.

"No way."

"We can't," he said.

"Why not?"

"Lots of reasons. For one thing I can't go out alone after it's dark. My mom won't let me."

"So what?" I asked.

"That means we can't do it," Eric answered.

"Wrong," I said.

"Wrong?"

"We just get our coats and go out the front door," I said. "Melissa and Crystal are baking cookies. You know they never come down to the playroom since they got grown up. Your mom is fixing up Karl's room, right?"

He nodded. "She's painting it. Karl is sharing with me for a couple of days. He's already in bed. It's a real pain. In the middle of the night he always . . . "

I stopped him. "Tell me this later. Let's go read the date book first."

He shook his head. "I don't want to go."

"Chicken," I said.

"Am not."

"Are too."

"Am not."

"Are too."

"I'm not chicken. It's just that my mom never lets me go out by myself when it's dark. I don't want to do stuff behind her back."

"You're not going out alone," I told him. "You'll be with me."

He thought about that. "I don't think you count. She means with her or Crystal."

"Did she say that?" I asked him.

"No."

"So you can come with me," I said.

"But I always tell her where I'm going," he insisted.

"Well, this time you can't," I told him. "You can't because it'll give away my secret."

"I don't know . . . "

"If you don't go, then I'll go alone," I said.

"You'd go by yourself?" he asked.

"Sure. Would you let your best friend go

alone?" I asked him.

"I don't know ..."

"We'll be back in half an hour. Honest. And if your mom finds out I'll take the blame," I promised.

"You will?"

"Sure. I'll tell her I knocked you over the head and you went crazy for a half hour and I could make you do anything I wanted."

"She won't believe that stupid story," he said.

"Please," I said. "Please. For me."

"Okay," he said. "But I don't like it."

Phew, I thought. That was hard work. I was glad he agreed to go with me. There was no way I could have gone alone. I would have been too scared.

There was no problem sneaking out his back door. We didn't see anybody on the five-minute walk to school.

"This is fun, huh?" I asked as we got to the school.

"No, it isn't," Eric said. "It's sort of scary. Let's go home."

"But we're here. It'll just take a minute to look at the book. Then we'll go."

I started walking toward the front door. Eric grabbed my arm to stop me.

"Does the key only work on the front doors?" he asked.

"No. It works on all of them," I told him. "Why?"

"There's cars driving by," he said. "What if someone sees us going in the front door and thinks we're breaking in? What if they call the police?"

"Right." I nodded. "We don't want the cops here, do we?"

"My mom would kill me if I came home in a police car," Eric said. "Come to think of it, she's going to kill me anyway. As soon as she finds out."

"She isn't going to find out," I said. "Ten minutes from now, we'll be in your basement again. Let's go around the back."

We moved around the playground side. And, all of a sudden, I got spooked. I wanted to run home. Just take off and run the ten blocks at full speed.

There wasn't anything to scare me. It was just the feeling I got being at the back of the school.

In the dark.

Two spotlights lit up the schoolyard, but they weren't that bright. The slides and swings were just black, scary shapes. Shadows. They looked an awful lot like monsters.

"Why did you stop?" Eric asked.

"You don't think there are monsters back here, do you?" I asked.

"Why do you say that? Are you trying to scare me? If you are, then it's working. You're making me feel weird, Selby. Let's go back to my place."

It sounded like a great idea. I was about to agree with him. But then a little voice in the back of my head said, "You're being silly, Selby. There's no such thing as monsters. You're almost nine years old. Nine! That's much, much too old to believe in monsters."

So I took a deep breath. Then I tried to blow the fear out of me.

"What are you doing?" Eric wanted to know. "Why are you breathing like that?"

"No reason," I told him. "Yeah, I was trying to scare you when I asked about monsters. You know there's no such thing, right?"

"Right," he said.

"Don't be silly then." I was surprised how brave I sounded. I sounded as if I believed what I was saying.

Only part of me did.

I put the key in the lock and turned it. I pulled the door open.

Eric and I went from a dark schoolyard into a darker school.

Chapter 10

Something in the Boiler Room

"**W**hy is it so dark in here?" Eric whispered.

"I don't know," I whispered back.

I'd never been in the school at night when there was nobody else in it. I'd been there for plays and concerts and Brownies. Then all the lights had been turned on. It was really bright.

Now there were only a couple of lights on. Just enough to make the hallway look spooky.

"How come all the lights are off?" Eric asked softly.

"Why would they leave them on? There's no one here but us. And why are you whispering?"

"I don't know," he said. "This is weird, Selby. It seems like someplace else. It doesn't seem like school."

"Come on," I said. "Let's go read the date book."

Our footsteps thumped and clumped down the big empty hall.

As we passed the library door, Brian Butz's stupid story popped into my head. I started thinking about a Grat . . . the monster that lives in the boiler room.

What was it Brian had said? "Maybe a Grat will eat you someday."

We were coming to the boiler room. I was spooked to see an open door. There was a weak light shining into the hall.

I stopped.

"What's up?" Eric asked.

I was about to tell him that there was a monster in the boiler room. But I didn't. The little voice made me act brave.

"There's a light in the boiler room," I said.

Eric inched closer to the door. I guess he didn't remember what I told him about Grats.

"Be careful," I said.

He poked his head around the open doorway and peeked in. I got all tensed up. I was ready to run as soon as he shouted, "There's a monster in there!"

But he didn't. He just turned to me and smiled. "I don't see anything," he said.

We kept walking, getting closer to the office.

"I feel braver now," Eric told me.

"Good," I said.

I don't, I thought.

"Nobody in class is going to believe we did this," he said.

"We can't ever tell them," I pointed out. "It's got to be our secret."

"Wow! Look at that!" Eric said so loud that it made me jump.

"What?"

"Look at all the bake stuff. Doesn't it look great?"

I let my breath out between my teeth. Then I slapped him on the arm.

"Ow," he said. "What was that for?"

"Because you almost gave me a heart attack. That's what. Don't shout!"

"You're shouting now," he said.

"Am not."

"Are too."

"Am not."

"Are too."

"I am not," I said. "I'm just trying to tell you that you scared me."

"Sorry," he said. "But look at the good stuff on the tables."

It did look great. The tables Mr. Musgrove had set up were covered with all kinds of neat-looking things. Plastic-wrapped cakes, pies, tarts and cookies waited for the bake sale tomorrow.

Eric pointed to a plate. "Blueberry tarts," he said. "I love blueberry tarts. Do you think I could take one now and pay for it tomorrow?"

"How would you explain that?" I asked.

"Oh, yeah."

And then we heard it. A strange noise. A noise coming from the boiler room. It was a low, shuffling sound. Something was moving, way at the back.

"What's that?" Eric asked. His voice came out in a squeak.

"Something's coming," I squeaked back.

"Something?"

The sound got louder. It shuffled closer to the doorway. The light that was shining from the boiler room half-vanished. Something was casting a shadow. The shadow got bigger and bigger. The noise got louder and louder.

"What is it?" Eric said in his squeaky voice.

I knew what it was. It couldn't be anything else. It had to be a Grat.

And I was right. Something with a big, hairy head stepped into the hallway. It turned to face us.

"Monster!" I yelled. It wasn't really a yell — more like a screech.

Eric and I turned and charged down the hall.

The only problem was, we forgot about the tables in the way. Tables full of baked stuff.

"Ooof!" I moaned as I hit the first table at tummy level. I bounced off and fell.

"Oooof!" Eric groaned as he hit the table. He didn't fall. He went sailing forward into the cakes and pies.

I tried to stand up. The monster would be chasing us. We had to run away.

I got to my hands and knees. At the same time, Eric knocked a chocolate cake off the table. It landed on my head with a soft thump.

Plastic wrap, cake and icing slid slowly across my face. I wiped at the icky mess and blinked away the goo.

Then something grabbed my arm and pulled me to my feet. Through the cake and icing I saw Eric. If I hadn't been so scared, I would have laughed. He was covered with pieces of pies and cakes. There were cherries in his hair. White icing made a mask on his face. Parts of squashed cupcakes and tarts hung on his jacket.

"It's coming," Eric yelled at me.

I turned around. The hairy monster was walking toward us, getting closer and closer.

We started running again. I slipped on the rest of the chocolate cake, but Eric grabbed me and kept me from falling.

We ran down the hall at full speed. I think we could have made it out the door in time. We could have beat the monster. But ahead of us, the office door opened.

Another Grat walked into the hall.

Chapter 11

Monsters in
the School

"ARRGGHH!" I screamed.

The Grats stopped. The two dark shapes looked at us. Neither one moved. Maybe they were thinking of the best way to eat us.

Out of the corner of my eye I saw Eric pull something off the wall. When I turned around he was holding the fire extinguisher.

"I saw this in a movie," he told me.

Then he began to spray foamy stuff over the office monster. The Grat made an awful, growly sound as the foam hit it in the face. Then it fell backward. It landed with a thud on the floor.

"Whoopee!" Eric shouted.

I can be just as brave, I thought. I can fight back too.

I ran to the baked goods. The other Grat stood at the far end of the tables. It didn't charge at me. Maybe it was surprised that Eric had sprayed its friend.

I picked up an apple pie and flung it at the monster. It landed in the middle of its chest: *tha-dump.*

"Hey, what the . . . " the Grat cried.

I never knew monsters could talk.

I grabbed a plate of iced cupcakes and pulled off the plastic wrap. I threw them at the monster's head, one at a time. The first one hit it right on the nose. The Grat lifted its arms to stop my cupcake bombs.

"Stop . . . " it called.

I sneaked a quick look over my shoulder. I couldn't see all that well in the weak light, but I did see that Eric was moving toward his monster. The Grat was covered in piles of foam.

I ripped the waxed paper off a plate of cookies. I threw them at the Grat like little Frisbees. A couple bounced off its head.

"Hey," the Grat shouted. "Stop that, man."

I took hold of a large raisin bun. Man? I thought. That's a funny way for a monster to talk.

"Is that you, Selby?" the Grat called.

"Oh no," I said to myself. "I know that voice. It's not a monster." I dropped the bun on the table.

"Is that you, Selby?" Mr. Musgrove asked again. I watched him walk toward me. He didn't move too quickly. I guess he thought I might throw another pie.

As he got closer, I saw the bushy moustache. He didn't have his long hair tied in a ponytail. It was as bushy as his moustache. That's why he'd looked so hairy.

"Hello, Mr. Musgrove," I said. "What are you doing here?"

"I work here," he told me. "What are you doing here?"

I didn't know what to say.

"How come you wrecked all the baked stuff?" he wanted to know.

"I thought you were a Grat?" I said.

"Huh? What are you talking about, man? And who's that?" Mr. Musgrove pointed down the hall.

"That's Eric," I said.

"Who's the other guy?" he asked.

The other monster was trying to stand up. Twice he slipped in the foam. The second time he smacked his head on the floor.

"Ouch," Mr. Musgrove and I said at the same time.

Then the front doors to Spruce Grove School flew open, and someone else marched in. He reached for the light switch. Suddenly it was so bright I had to blink.

Dad stood with his hands resting on his hips. He looked at me. Then at Mr. Musgrove. Then at Eric and the foamy shape moaning on the floor. Then at the wiped-out bake tables.

"What is going on here?" he demanded.

"Thank goodness you're safe," my mom said as she ran past Dad. I think she was going to give me a hug, but the chocolate cake I was wearing stopped her. "Why are you covered in cake?" she asked.

Eric's mom was there too. She ran to Eric with her arms out. Then she saw the goo all over him. She ended up patting his shoulder.

"What a mess," Melissa said as she came into the hall.

Then I saw two policemen standing with Dad. They were looking around with angry stares.

"All right," one of the cops said. "Somebody tell us what's going on." He pointed at Mr. Musgrove. "Who are you?"

"I'm the janitor, man," Mr. Musgrove said. "I was working at the back of the boiler room. I had my Walkman on, but I thought I heard people talking. When I came out I saw these three. Then one of them started to throw cakes and cookies at me."

The cop pointed at me. "Is that your daughter?" he asked my dad.

"Yes," he said. "And this is her best friend, Eric. He's the one who wrote the note."

"The note?" I wondered.

"I left a note on the time machine," Eric told me. "I left a note saying that we'd gone to the school to read your Dad's book."

"Why did you do that?" I asked.

"I didn't want my mom to worry if she went into the playroom and found us gone," he answered.

His mother patted his shoulder again.

"That's how come you're here?" I asked.

Melissa nodded. "Crystal and I went down to look at the time machine and found the note. Her mom called the folks. Mom called the police just in case. It's too bad Crystal can't be here to see this mess. She got stuck babysitting Karl."

"It was such a stupid, stupid thing to do," Mom said. "We were so worried. How many times have I told you to tell us where you are, all the time."

"I wanted you to listen to me," I told her. I felt wetness around my eyes. "I'm sorry. I know it

was wrong. I just wanted you to listen to me at Bugging Time. I'm tired of being the little kid."

Tears ran down my face and across the chocolate cake. I tasted salty, sweet icing.

Mom hugged me. Even though I was making a mess of her coat, she pulled me tightly against her chest. "Oh, honey," she said. "I was so worried. I love you very, very much."

"And who's this?" The cop pointed at the foamy shape.

I tried to wipe my eyes so I could see the other Grat. With the lights turned on, I knew who it was.

"That's the man who set up the new computer today," Dad said. "What is he doing here?"

"That's a good question," the cop said. "A very good question."

Chapter 12

Dumb,
Lucky Heroes

Eric and I sat in the middle of the time machine on Saturday afternoon.

"It's still hard to believe that we caught a real robber," Eric said.

"Yeah," I agreed. "Who would have thought that the computer guy would be breaking into our school? Who would have thought he'd try to steal the new computer?"

"Or that he'd hear us and get scared," Eric said.

"The police told my dad they found lots of

other computer stuff he stole. The cops said he'd been doing it for months. He'd set up a computer then think of the best way to break in and steal it."

"That's called casing the joint," Eric told me. "I saw it on TV."

"Who would think the same guy who sold you the computer would steal it back."

"You think they'll give us medals and stuff?" Eric asked. "It's not every day that third grade kids catch a robber."

"No way," I said. "My folks were so mad I'm lucky they didn't ground me until I'm a grandmother."

Eric laughed. "You know, Selby," he said. "In a way, we're heroes."

"Not really. We're just dumb and lucky," I said. "We shouldn't have been out alone. That guy could have done anything. What if we had walked in on him in the office? What if Mr. Musgrove hadn't been there? What if you hadn't left the note? We were really dumb. And we're lucky it worked out the way it did."

"Okay, so we're dumb, lucky heroes," Eric said.

That made us laugh too.

"I feel kind of bad about it now," I said. "My mom and dad were really worried."

"My mom too," he said.

Karl poked his head into the time machine. "Can I play?" he asked.

"No," Eric told him. "Go away."

"Show me your underwear."

"Go away," Eric said.

"How are you going to make me?" Karl asked.

"If you don't go, I'll grab you and I'll show your underwear to Selby," Eric said.

Karl thought about that for a few seconds. "Bye," he said.

We laughed.

"Say, Selby, did you think that Mr. Musgrove and the other guy were real monsters?" Eric asked.

I nodded. "I thought we were being attacked by a couple of Grats."

"My mom says that there's no such things as Grats," he said.

"My folks say the same thing."

"They know, huh?"

"They know," I agreed. "But it doesn't mean much when you get in a dark place, does it? I mean when it's dark and spooky, you think scary things."

"How are you going to get your family to listen to you now?" Eric wondered. "Now that they know about the date book thing."

"We made a deal," I said. "They promised not to treat me like a little kid. I promised not to do anything stupid again."

"That sounds good."

"We'll see. Melissa still left the top off the toothpaste today."

"What?"

"It's a thing of hers," I said. "You want to go play outside?"

"It's too cold," he said. "Let's play time machine."

"All right. When do you want to go to?"

"The only time I don't want to go to is last night," he said.

"You know, you looked pretty stupid last night," I told him. "You had cherries in your hair."

"So? You had chocolate cake all over your face. You looked stupider than I did."

"Did not."

"Did too."

"Did not."

"Did too."

Of course, we had to laugh at that too.

Martyn Godfrey was born in England in 1949, but he spent most of his childhood in Toronto. Writing did not come easily to Martyn at first. In fact, he had to repeat the third grade because he had so much trouble with Language Arts. He went to teacher's college in Toronto, and worked as a teacher for eleven years before he quit to become a full-time writer.

Martyn wrote his first book when one of his sixth grade students challenged him to write a space story. That story became the first draft of *The Day the Sky Exploded*. He went on to write more than a dozen popular and award-winning books for young readers, including the *Ms Teeny-Wonderful* books and *Do You Want Fries With That?*